make~a~wish

*For Daniel*
~ the inspiration for this book ~
who strongly believed in sharing.
Love you for ever and ever, Mummy.

And with greatest thanks
to all the contributors
for sharing their wishes
with us all.

# Make a Wish

I wish, I wish, I wish . . .

*'I can remember when I was a child*
*that my bed was a ship*
*and I sailed through the night . . .'*

This enchanting line from a 1960s song so encapsulates the power and magic of children's dreams.

How many times a day do you say, "I wish . . ."? We all have wishes – and some of them even come true. How memorable it is when they do!

This book has been lovingly created to celebrate the work of Make-a-Wish Foundation®, a charity that imaginatively uses its wish-making powers to grant wishes to very sick children all around the world. The wishes touch the children's lives with that special ray of light at a moment when it is so greatly needed, at the same time helping to make wonderful memories for them and their families.

This volume contains contributions by many stars from the universe of children's books, whose work is well-known and well-loved all over the world by thousands of children and adults alike. They have been generous enough to share their wishes with us.

Wishes can be simple, they can be fantastical, they can be fun! We wish for wonderful experiences, for possessions, to go to magical places. We invited our contributors to unfetter their imaginations, and their exciting thoughts and ideas are here for us all to enjoy. We hope this book will release your imaginations, too!

Have you ever asked your loved ones what they wish for?

And if you could wish
            for anything you wanted . . .
                        what would your wish be?

these wishes are from . . .

"I wish I could play among the clouds."

"I wish
    I could find
        a secret door."

I wish I could have chocolate
Whenever it's time to eat –
For breakfast, lunch and tea I think
Would be a lovely treat.

I wish I could have a pudding,
An enormous cloudy dream
Of cheesecake and gateau and sweet lollipops
Dripping with double whipped cream.

And when it was time for snacks and breaks
I'd have some fudge or gooey cakes.
It may seem a greedy thing to do
But, of course,

I'd always share with you!

"I wish I could fly."

# I wish I was a leopard!

I wish I was a leopard!
I'd gobble up three bullies,
(or maybe four)
and then I'd run off
really quickly
before anyone found out it was me.

*Rahhhhh!*

At night, I'd prowl and sing with the little cats.
We'd hold concerts
under the stars

*Meeeowooo!*

*La la la!*

*Bravo!*

*Grrrrrr!*

I'd eat at the finest restaurants
and if a snooty waiter said,
"You can't have animals in here,"
I'd gobble him up too.

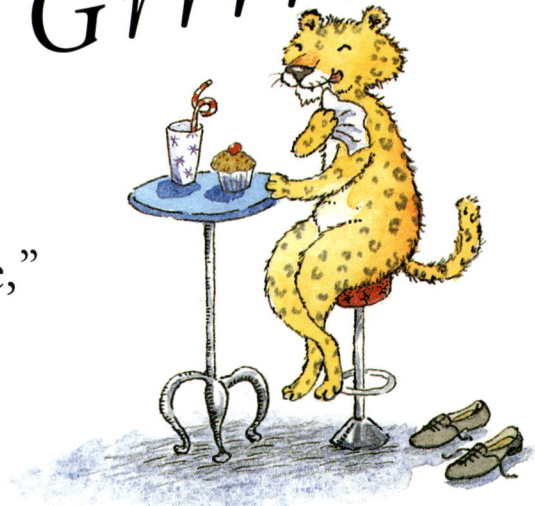

I'd roar at old ladies and at small babies

*Hee hee hee!*

And then, when I was all done
with growling and prowling,
I'd find a nice warm place
and purr
and purr
and

*Purrrrrrrr!*

I wish I were a cat,

I really fancy that.

"I wish I could ride a dinosaur."

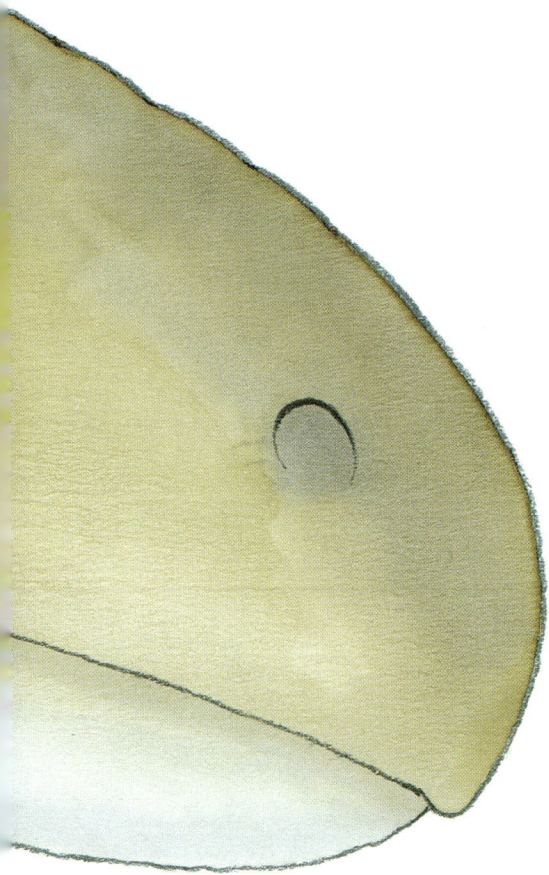

Sally O'Mally went to the zoo.
She played hopscotch with a kangaroo.
She slid with the seals,
She hid with the bears,

She jumped with the penguins
Up and down stairs.

Then Sally O'Mally
made her mistake.
She decided to
skip with
a snake.
Do you wish you
could play in a zoo, too?

Hiss! Gulp! Silly Sally.

"I wish I was a super-hero!"

"I wish
I could
WASH
like an elephant –

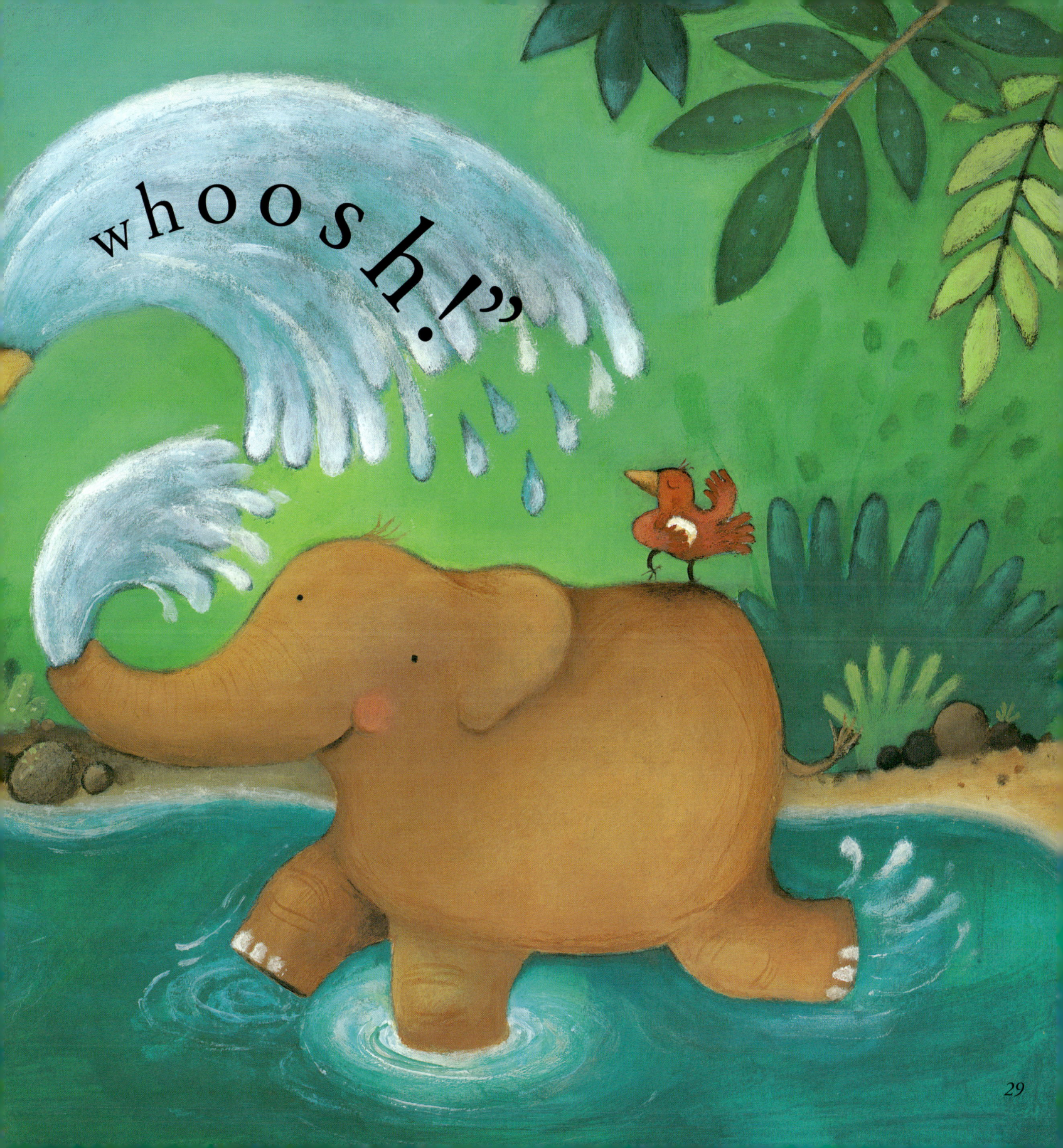

whoosh!"

THINKS
OH, HOW I WISH THAT GUMDROP COULD WIN AT SILVERSTONE! BUT I KNOW ONLY TOO WELL THAT HE WASN'T BUILT TO GO VERY FAST.
BIRO '02

HA-HA,
THAT'S BECAUSE
I'VE ACTIVATED THE
SECRET SWITCH
AGAIN. WOOF-WOOF!

Just the same, Mr Oldcastle had a go.
And then – to his utter amazement and delight –
Gumdrop won the race outright!

"I wish
    I could sleep
        on swansdown."

When I was out yesterday
What did I see?
A flittery fairy –
I asked her to tea.
I wanted three wishes –
She fluttered her wings
And warned me that wishes
Are tricksical things.

I thanked her politely, I said it was fine – I wanted those wishes!
Those wishes were MINE!

*But -*

I wished for a fish
And she gave me a shark.
I wanted a boat
And she gave me an ark.

So now I can't paddle
For maybe – who knows?
That shark will come swooshing
And nibble my toes.

And all of the animals
Grumble all day.
The donkeys want thistles
The horses want hay.
The monkeys are moaning
The hippos are groaning
The tigers are growling
Hyenas are howling –
The elephants stamping
The lions are roaring

And only the wombat is peacefully snoring.

It's such a commotion out here on the ocean.
It goes on all night and it goes on all day –
I wish that they'd all of them just GO AWAY –

*Ooops!*

a friendly smile and shining eyes
with a splash in the sparkling blue

the flick of a tail
and curving fin
with a splash
in the sparkling blue

twists and turns fast and slow
with a splash in the sparkling blue

out in the sea through the gentle waves
with a splash
in the sparkling blue

I wish I could swim
with a dolphin
with a splash
in the sparkling blue

"I wish I had a treasure map."

High in the sky

Whirling **around**.

Two *reckless* rabbits

Up-side-down!

I wish

I wish

I wish

I wish

I wish

I wish that I could fly.

"I wish I could visit
Father Christmas
in the land of snow."

"I wish I was a cowboy in the wild, wild west."

"I wish
I was a
fireman,
rushing to
the rescue."

47

Called a soapbox (says the Dad),
Kinda go-kart (says his lad),
How we wish we could win a race

But we really wish it were a rocket
Zooming into outer . . .

49

"I wish
I could make
friends
with a
giraffe."

"I wish I were a Rock 'n' Roll star."

What would your wish be?

*picture by Tiffany Leeson   p8~9*

*Helen Oxenbury   p13*

*Nick Butterworth   p14~15*

*Candice Whatmore   p16~17*

*Ian Beck   p18~19*

Jan Fearnley  p20~21

Nick Sharratt p22~23

Mick Inkpen    p24~25

words by Pippa Goodhart  pictures by Jennie Maizels   p26

Jess Meserve    p27

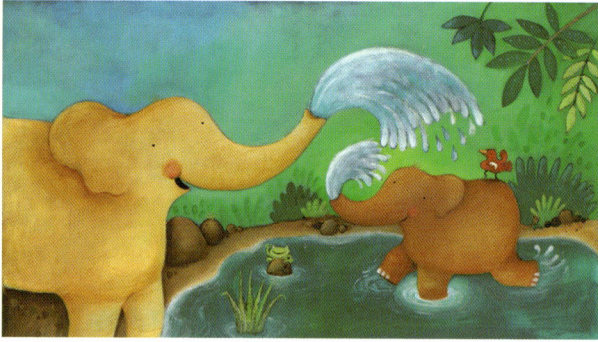

words by Julia Donaldson  picture by Lucy Richards  p28~29

Val Biro   p30~31

Claire Fletcher   p32~33

words by Vivian French  pictures by Sue Heap  p34~35

Rebecca Elgar   p36~37

Tony Ross   p38

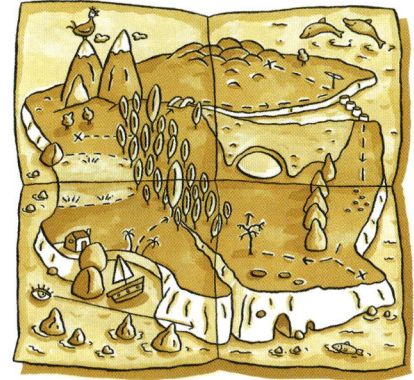

Ant Parker   p39

Mike Bostock   p40~41

Mary Murphy   p42~43

Michael  Foreman   p44~45

Alison Bartlett   p46

Caroline Mockford   p47

Korky Paul   p48~49

Lydia Monks   p50~51

Paul Howard  p52

# make~a~wish

Make-A-Wish Foundation® has a very simple objective – to turn the wishes of children aged between 3 and 18, living with life-threatening illnesses, into reality. A wish granted is true magic for children and provides many happy memories for them and for their families.

Make-A-Wish Foundation® is the largest wish-granting organisation in the world and was originally formed in Phoenix, Arizona in 1980. There are now 22 affiliates throughout the world, all liaising closely with each other when a child wishes to visit their country. The countries include America, Australia, Austria, Canada, Chile, Denmark, France, Greece, Hong Kong, India, Israel, Japan, Mexico, the Philippines and the United Kingdom to name but a few.

Today a child enjoys a Make-A-Wish® experience at the rate of one wish per hour, every day around the world.

*Visit the website at www.make-a-wish.org.uk*
*Charity Registration no. 295672*

The authors and illustrators have generously contributed their work without charge for the benefit of Make-A-Wish Foundation® UK. Egmont Books Limited will pay to Make-A-Wish Foundation® the royalties foregone by each of the contributors and will donate a matching amount. Egmont anticipates that around 20% of net monies received by it from the sale of this book will be paid to Make-A-Wish Foundation®.

*With thanks to all the authors and illustrators who made this book possible:*

*pp8-9 © 2002 Tiffany Leeson*
*p13 © 2002 Helen Oxenbury*
*pp14-15 © 2002 Nick Butterworth*
*pp16-17 © 2002 Candice Whatmore*
*pp18-19 © 2002 Ian Beck*
*pp20-21 © 2002 Jan Fearnley*
*pp22-23 © 2002 Nick Sharratt*
*pp24-25 © 2002 Mick Inkpen*
*p26 text © 2002 Pippa Goodhart*
*illustrations © 2002 Jennie Maizels*
*p27 © 2002 Jess Meserve*
*p28-29 text © 2002 Julia Donaldson*
*illustration © 2002 Lucy Richards*
*pp30-31 © 2002 Val Biro*
*pp32-33 © 2002 Claire Fletcher*
*pp34-35 text © 2002 Vivian French*
*illustrations © 2002 Sue Heap*
*pp36-37 © 2002 Rebecca Elgar*
*p38 © 2002 Tony Ross*
*p39 © 2002 Ant Parker*
*pp40-41 © 2002 Mike Bostock*
*pp42-43 © 2002 Mary Murphy*
*pp44-45 © 2002 Michael Foreman*
*p46 © 2002 Alison Bartlett*
*p47 © 2002 Caroline Mockford*
*pp48-49 © 2002 Korky Paul*
*pp50-51 © 2002 Lydia Monks*
*p52 © 2002 Paul Howard*

*All the authors and illustrators have asserted their moral rights*

*p8 MYSTERIOUS PEOPLE* Words and Music by Beppe Wolgers and Olle Adolphson, English language translation of original song *(Det Gatfulla Folket)* by Hal Shaper © 1959, Reuter & Reuter Musikforlags, Sweden Reproduced by permission of Robbins Music Corp Ltd, London WC2H 0QY

This edition published in Great Britain 2002
by Egmont Books Limited
239 Kensington High Street, London W8 6SA

A CIP catalogue record for this title
is available from the British Library

Printed and bound in Italy

10 9 8 7 6 5 4 3 2 1

ISBN 14052 0178 9